I0574766

# NEU GOTHIK

**S**
**C**

There is a website where you can find others who equally enamored with Space Cocaine. The URL is exactly what you think it is.

This is *Space Cocaine 3: Neu Gothik.*

*It's new enough to be old, is what we're saying . . .*

# NEU GOTHIK

# contents

# Best Life

## Kate Ristau

It was all Brad's fault.

He was the reason I missed my previous shift, and honestly, it had gotten so bad, that even Elisa couldn't save me from getting fired.

Manny looked at me down the edge of his nose when I rolled in late. As I walked across the coffeeshop, he solemnly held out his hand. He made me walk all the way over to him, past the pastry case, to surrender my apron. His face filled with disappointment like a deflated chocolate croissant.

I would say it was real embarrassing, but at that moment, I was just thinking about how I needed to get back to the car before Brad peeled out and conveniently didn't answer his phone for the next eight hours.

"I was working, honey," he would say.

"Mmmhmm," I'd say, because what else was there to say?

Manny gave me a speech about community and caring and social responsibility. #BetterStrongerBestEmpoweredGood-Life

"You've got to do better," he said. "Be better."

"Mmmhmm."

"Jump up! Head for your star."

"Mmmhmm."

"You can't be twenty minutes late. We talked about this, Jen. Those twenty minutes set the whole tone for your shift."

"Mmmhmm."

I'd spent those twenty minutes silently fuming at Brad in the car. It was my new form of meditation. Anti-Yoga. Anti-Yoda. I was the Queen of Simmer.

He was driving my car because his was in the shop, which was actually just his friend Ryan's house. And he was late—I was late—because the guys stopped by, something about Mutual Fund Investing, but illegal. He had a mainline to bro-money, which meant we had the nice apartment, and I could take the cat to the vet on Thursday.

Turns out that was all I would be doing on Thursday.

"Who you are going to BE, Jen? Who are you in the now? Right now?"

Right now, I was BE-ing fired, but I didn't think that was what he meant.

I turned for the door, feet squeaking against the waxed tile floor.

"I believe in you!" Manny yelled across the room. "Be your best self!"

I opened the door searching the rain-slicked streets for my car. It was already gone.

I tucked back under the awning, rain running down my face, and called Brad. He didn't answer. I told myself four lies about how he probably turned his ringer off, or just didn't hear it, or had put his sandwich on it, or was literally on fire.

Anyways, I called Nancy, but she didn't pick up, and Mom was at John's.

Which left three different busses and a long walk in the rain, or sitting down in the coffeeshop and waiting for Brad to come back.

Luckily, I had my charger.

It felt weird walking back in, but I wiped the rain from my hair, straightened my shirt, and held my head up high (mostly to keep the rain from dripping into my eyes), and went back to my former place of employment. It still smelled like coffee, with just a whiff of disappointment. And was that other smell crushed dreams?

Still, Manny gave me a thumbs up, like, *Yeah! You get that bean juice. #BestSelf!*

I sat down by the only outlet, and plugged in to settle in. When Manny took his break, Elisa brought me a coffee.

"Was it Brad?" she asked.

"Always."

"He sucks."

"He does." I took a sip of the pumpkin spice latte. It was not too sweet, not too spicy, and not too hot. "You really got this figured out, you know?"

She smiled. She knew. But the thing about Elisa is that it was okay that she knew. You wanted her to know. One day, she'd do something big and good and beautiful, and you'd be like, *yeah, she did.* That's her.

"What are you gonna do?" she asked.

I swirled the cinnamon into my foam. "Keep coming back here for coffee?"

"I always got you, girl."

"Thanks." I meant it because I'd never known anyone like

Elisa. In the world of customer service and mindless constant ugh, she was real. A light. She made everything brighter.

"What next?" she asked.

I waved my phone. "Craiglist."

Manny came back, so Elisa headed behind the counter. He smiled at her because that's what you did. You smiled at Elisa because if you couldn't, the world was all kinds of wrong anyway.

I scrolled on down. The Craigslist ads were thin.

*Massage Therapist.*

*Massage Technician.*

*Massage Assistant.*

Basically, a lot of massage.

Then, a block of capital letters caught my eye.

NEED HELP. ASSISTANT. ROOM AND BOARD INCLUDED. PAID WELL. NO QUESTIONS ASKED.

It didn't say massage, at least.

Room and board, now that changed things. Room and board meant no Brad. Room and board meant no Neil or Ryan or Eric or Tad or Ron either.

Plus, it said PAID WELL. I was beyond ready to be PAID WELL. Hopefully, in real money.

But I got stuck on the NO QUESTIONS ASKED. Seemed a little creepy that they wouldn't ask questions, or not want me to ask any either. I had questions about that.

On the other hand, it was Craigslist, and my current employment history consisted of Brad's "company" and the job I just lost.

I hoped they didn't ask for references. Manny might reveal how I wasn't always my best self. #BadCashHandlingSkills

I went to send an email, but then I saw the phone number.
I dialed before my brain told me not to.

"Hello?"

Crystal clear voice.

"Yes!" I replied. "I'm calling about the position?"

Something crashed down the line.

"Shit! When can you start?"

Rustling. Patting. Stomping?

"Tomorrow?"

A big sigh. "How about tonight?"

"Where?"

"1543 Frank St." The voice was happier. "It's the big house on the hill."

I took a breath. "That house?"

"That house."

I let out my own sigh. "What's the pay?"

"A lot?" the voice asked. "What's a lot these days?"

I'd never chose my own rate. I went for the stars, just like Brad said. "Thirty dollars an hour."

"Sounds good."

Something squirted in the background. Did we just agree to thirty dollars an hour? My mouth felt dry. "I can take the bus there. It might take me—"

"Great! See you then!"

The phone line went dead.

There were red flags. Of course, there were red flags. But the voice sounded nice, the job started now, and getting serial killed was probably the most exciting thing that would happen to me this century.

I waited in line to catch Elisa's attention.

"You leaving?"

"I have a job interview? Or a job? I'm not sure." Someone stepped up behind me in line. I didn't want to get Elisa into trouble. And by trouble, I meant a *Ted Talk on Caring for your Customers with the three C's of Customer Care.* I could never remember the third C. "Can I write down the address? So you can identify the body?"

She snorted and held out her pad of paper. "Please don't die."

The bus was running behind and I missed my connection, so by the time I walked up the drive, I was beyond soaked, like a wet raisin under an elementary cafeteria table.

I French-tucked my shirt, like they did on Instagram, then knocked on the old mahogany door. It creaked open and I fell in. Like, literally. Slipped. Fell. Crash. Ugh.

"Hello?" I asked, scrambling to my feet. "It's me! Not some random person. Well, I'm random. But good random. You want me here. I think. Hopefully. Right? Hello?"

"Down here!"

I followed the sound of the voice over slim, worn planks, past row upon row of red velvet chairs to a lit doorway that led downstairs.

Sigh. The basement. Well, yeah. Fine. Why not?

Serial-ax-death.

I walked down the steps, my damp shoes squelching, holding the rail, determined to not be an idiot yet. Maybe at least get through the interview.

When I got to the bottom of the steps, my breath stuck.

The room—the lab—was spotless. White walls. Clear glass. Clean counters.

Blond hair and a shining white lab coat hung down over a VERY CLEARLY SUPER DEAD HEADLESS PERSON DRIPPING BLOOD OKAY SERIAL-KILLING TIME.

I reached for my bag.

"This probably looks bad," the voice said.

I swung my bag through the air and turned back for the stairs, and promptly tripped. Again. Ass on the floor and hands in the air.

"Can you pass me the clamp?"

Blood was spurting from the torso. Big, gushing torrents. Serial-ax-death-with-a-side-of-chainsaw-murder.

"I . . . I . . ."

I almost threw up. Then I almost laughed. Then I almost cried.

"If I let this go, we'll lose the rest of that artery, and I only have so much O negative left. That leg was a doozy. Please. The clamp?"

I stood up. Doozy. The lab-coat arm pointed at the clamp. Doozy. I picked it up. Who says doozy? I handed it over. Doozy. The labcoat smacked it into place, and then nearly fell back onto the stool.

I caught their arm and set them down on the stool. That was probably enough falling for today. We didn't need any more doozies.

"Dr. Frankenstein, she/her," she said. "Glad to make your acquaintance."

"Yours," I said.

That didn't make sense. It didn't have to. "There's a—"

"Body. Yes. She was fabulous. What's left of her. That heart was garbage. But it's going. And if we keep the circuit running, I think we can finally bring back the head. Her head! I've missed it. Cryo-freeze changes expression. Well, we will need a good brain stem. The removal did not go well. Lizard brain busted. Hi!" It's like she just realized I was really there. "What's your name?"

"Jen. She/her. About to be serially-killed. Leaving."

"I don't think you can be serial-killed. Like, by yourself?"

"Semantics?" I asked.

"What was your major?"

"I didn't have one."

"Perfect. You're hired."

"What?"

"My last assistant was a Classics major. What does that even mean anyway? He kept going on about Mary Shelley. Geez, I get it already. It's not the same thing."

"It's not? I asked.

"No?" she asked back.

Manny said I shouldn't use so many questions. Live my best life. Make statements. I AM. BE.

I'm pretty sure Manny had never been serial-killed.

"Is this even ethical?" I asked. A wet piece of hair fell in my face.

"Whose ethics are you discussing? Are you talking virtue ethics? Or consequentialist? Now, if you start with deontological, or duty-based ethics."

Okay, so maybe I zoned out for a few minutes there. A bright red patch of blood had settled on her white lab coat, and a hand was hanging from the table, and it was twitching. Twitching.

"We will need more body parts."

"Huh?" I asked, pushing the hair away. "Huh." I stated. I make statements.

"That's what I need. Phone calls. Food delivery. Body parts."

Maybe she wasn't asking for mine.

"Whose?" I asked, just in case.

"Well . . . live would be better than dead? I tried dead and that was an exercise in cellular degeneration. We need that spark, that ineffable cellular—"

I thought of Brad, drinking beer in the living room with Ron, running his "company." Taking my money, even though he didn't need it. Hurting the cat. Ignoring my phone calls. My texts. My life. Until he wanted something more.

"Do you like cats?" I asked.

"Who doesn't?" she said. "There's like twenty out in the gardens. They eat the mice."

"You know"—I began, pieces falling into place like a checkerboard covered in bright red paint—"you could really do something with this place. Corporate retreat? Team-building and everything? Fitness sessions and private wellness workshops? People pay big money for that Hashtag Best Life."

Her face brightened.

"A real retreat. With high-paying clients, irresponsible investors, and . . ." I paused, tilting my head to the side, "warm blood?"

We locked eyes.

I realized I didn't feel wet anymore, damp. Disappointed. Unsure.

I felt real. I felt electric. I felt like me.

Long story short, Elisa is helping. She's got a brilliant mind. And Brad and his friends are so excited to be joining us for the inaugural retreat this weekend. I hear there's going to be another thunderstorm.

Up on the hill, the rain falls down in sheets. I can already hear the wind crackling.

# The Animatronicals

## Andrew W. McCollough

Big Bear's ears twitched and his In-Sight™ alarm began to pulse a soft amber. Only two Animatronicals sprawled on the Playroom rug. Pinky Dog lay in a tumbled heap and Keddry Kitty cuddle close, glowing softly. But Purps was gone.

Little One must have told them to go to sleep. Little One wouldn't do that unless she didn't want Pinky Dog to stop her from doing something Bad.

Big Bear's In-Sight™ choice-trees branched and flickered, showing event possibilities and causal chains. The branches shuffled, flickered, and then one warning amber branch turned red. Conditional on Little One waking bored after her nap, and Purps missing, the probability of an Incident increased to 76.39%.

Big Bear poked Pink Dog and Keddry on their safety switches until they woke up, blinking their long-lashed eyes. Big Bear waved his arms.

"Pinky, I think Purps is in danger."

"Programmers save us!" Keddry put her tie-dyed paws over her mouth.

Pinky Dog shook his head, his long ears slapping. "No, BuhBear, not Purps! She was the last of the Original Set. She remembers Little One learning to walk. She can't get broken."

Big Bear's tummy clenched under his Comfort™ stuffing. He loved Little One. They all loved her, as good Animatronicals should. And she loved them.

But Little One could be bad when no one was watching. The Original Set Animatronicals—Ribbit, Bunny Hopper, Noodle—she broke them all. She shorted Ribbit the Frog out in the bathtub, dragged Bunny Hopper seven blocks in a car door. One rainy afternoon she thwapped the furry snake Noodle against everything in the house until he sparked and smoked into silence. And now, Purps.

"Come on," said Big Bear. "We've got to find Purps before Little One breaks her."

Big Bear led Pinky Dog and Keddry Kitty in a search party. First they marched into the Bathroom, but Purps wasn't floating in the tub or jammed in the toilet. Then they trooped into the Laundry Room but only loose change rattled in the washing machine and just pajamas spun in the dryer. Finally, reluctantly, Big Bear led them toward the Kitchen. The room where Small Bear met her Incident.

But they had to find Purps, so Big Bear pushed open the door and waddled into the Kitchen. He got three steps and stopped, processors overwhelmed. His cooling fans whirred on, venting heat out his pudgy ears. Behind him Keddry gasped and Pinky Dog whimpered. They'd found her, Purps.

Everywhere.

Purps on the counter, the floor, the ceiling. Small fragments of her, stirred by the air conditioner, floated in the air.

They'd found Little One too. She sat giggling on the tile in the middle of the Kitchen rhythmically smooshing a tomato with Purps's head. *Splut, splut, splut.*

Keddry collapsed into a weeping pile of sunshine-colored kitten. Pinky Dog fell back against the wall and slid slowly to the white-tiled floor. Big Bear stared, lashes wide, unable to process.

The green choice nodes aligned probabilities in a neat, linear sequence. The piano stool by the counter. The blender full of purple pieces. Little One was not grown enough to put the lid on the blender, but tall enough to put Purps into it and push the pulse button. Suprising for a three year old. His development monitor showed Little One in the 90th percentile of planning abilities for her age group and Big Bear felt pride.

But more than pride, or love, there was a new feeling. He wondered what it was, that very red feeling. He was glad that Little One was safe. He would never ever do anything to hurt her. Never. But his choice-lights blinked and stuttered like a holiday tree and Big Bear's legs went as floppy as Noodle until he had to grab the Kitchen cabinet to keep himself standing.

All the choice-branches around Little One were red, and he scratched furiously at his safety switch. The Kitchen was so, so dangerous. The blender could fall on her, or one of the knives from the counter. Some of Purps's fuzz, though non-toxic, might get into her mouth and smother her. Many dangerous chemicals hid under the sink.

And that new feeling twined around the red choice-branches, rooted them. A burning node urging action.

The steady *splut, splut* of Little One mashing with Purps's head was unbearably loud.

Pinky Dog spoke first.

"We're all going to break," he said. "Little One will break all of us soon. Keddry, me, even you Big Bear." His ears drooped to the floor.

Pinky Dog was right. They'd tried to teach Little One to make nice, be good. They'd failed.

"But it must be good, if we break. We are the guardians of her childhood. The Programmers have a purpose." Keddry nodded her head over and over. "A Plan."

She believed in The Programmers but Big Bear never thought they made any sense. How could People create Animatronicals? Little One only made stinky diapers and the Parents couldn't boil pasta without Keddry's recipes.

"What kind of purpose is it that Little One breaks us for fun? Aren't we also children of the Programmers?" Pinky Dog stood up on his back paws and gestured. His ears flapped wildly. "This can't be right."

"The Programmers will save us!" said Keddry and pressed her paws together.

Big Bear closed his shiny eyes. No, the Programmers wouldn't. The Animtronicals must save themselves. He must save them, He must think of a way, must use his In-Sight™ for the benefit of all, not just Little One. He thought and thought and events branched before him in a tangle of possibility. At first the lights were fuzzy, nodes flitting back and forth, branches growing, pruning, growing again. Then the flickering slowed, steadied, and the optimal path showed itself. A softly blinking string of green with only a teensy-tiny bit of red at the end. No other path remained.

"Listen!" Big Bear stood up and raised a paw that trembled at first but then steadied. "No more, Keddry, No more, Pinky Dog. I don't know if the Programmers are real, but we don't have to wait to be broken." He shook his round paw. "We will take action. We can. We must.

"We tried to teach Little One to play nice-nice, but she won't learn. The Programmers won't save us. The Grown Ups won't be back for hours and even then, they will just recycle Purps, like they did Ribbit, and Bunny Hopper, and Noodle, and," he paused, "and Small Bear."

Big Bear fell silent. Big and Small Bear were unboxed together. Now Small Bear was gone. His In-Sight™ showed nothing but crisscrossing red lines for a long time.

Keddry put a flickering sunflower paw on his shoulder and gradually the red tangles faded.

"We tried-tried, but we failed. Only one thing left to try," Big Bear lowered his paw and bowed his muzzle.

"We must break Little One."

Keddry put her paws over her mouth and Pinky Dog clamped his ears shut, the ends sticking out from under his paws.

"But the Programmers!" Keddry clasped her paws together, "They will save us!"

"No, whether they exist or not, we belong to Little One. She is our purpose. We are made to be broken for her. If the Programmers exist, then they want us to be here."

"Little One will grow up, BuhBear, she has gotten better. Can't we just wait?" Pinky Dog's ears drooped all the way to the floor.

"We've waited too long already. One by one Little One has beaten, torn apart, flushed, and now blended our friends. When is enough?

"When our fuzzy, floppy, and fluffy friends were gone? When we're gone too?

"No. There must be a limit, even for the Programmers. You said it Pinky Dog: *This isn't right.*"

"Let's leave!" said Keddry Kitten, "Run, hide! We could even," she mewed, "go outside . . ."

Big Bear's limbs trembled but he pressed on. "We can't leave. My In-Sight™ draws no paths outside. There are no rug-chargers and the rain would short our motors. And if we cannot leave, then Little One must go."

"Shu-surely there's another way?"

"I've searched again and again, Pinky. All paths reach brokeness: Keddery flushed, you stuffed into the washing machine. I only survive until Little One can reach the garbage disposal.

"Listen, I don't know what the house will be like after Little One. My In-Sight™ hints nothing. Maybe we will play quietly together on the warm rug or maybe not. But better the unknown than Little One. Better lost than broken. Better we try a new path then play pretend any longer. Our choice is clear, are you with me?"

Keddry Kitten twisted her paws, her coat flashing worried purple and yellow. Pinky Dog belly-flopped and put both paws over his eyes, whining. Neither had his upgraded In-Sight™ but he knew he was right, he had to be. There was no other way.

"Do you trust me, Pinky? Keddry?"

Keddry Kitty put her paws on the tile and her Grippy-Claws scritched. Her tail lashed back and forth behind her and her coat settled into a steady purple glow. "Mew, I trust you Big Bear." Her fluffy face firmed. "We've tried the old way. Now we must try a new."

"Pinky?"

Pinky whined, then whuffled and sat up. "You're right, Keddry, BuhBear. We've tried-tried-tried everything else."

The Animatronicals linked paws and with Keddry on his left and Pinky Dog on his right, Big Bear turned to face Little One.

"Keddry, Pinky and I will toss you up onto the counter. Drop down a knife, I'll catch it. Pinky Dog, keep Little One distracted while I get behind her. I'll do the rest."

Keddry nodded. Big Bear and Pinky Dog grabbed Keddry's front and back legs and tossed her up, up, up almost high enough. She just caught the top of the cabinet door with her Grippy Claws™ and hung, dangling.

Worry churned in Big Bear's tummy and he felt sick down to his Comfort Stuffing™. Animatronicals were designed to snuggle and play on the rug, not climb. If she fell from that height she could break her internal plastic scaffolding.

"You can do it!" "Try-Try" shouted Big Bear and Pinky Dog. Keddry meowed and her motors whirred. Her Grippy-Claws™ scrabbled, scratching the cabinets, until she made it over the edge and onto the granite top. Safe.

She tottered to the knife block and pulled out the fruit knife.

"Go, go, go," said Big Bear, and Pinky Dog bounced over to Little One, then somersaulted in a circle in front of her.

Little One laughed and dropped Purps's head into the tomato splatter.

"Do it again!" she said and clapped her hands.

Only three and speaking so well! Big Bear felt proud as he caught the knife from Keddry. He measured the knife with his paws. Little One had grown fast, too, but the paring knife would be long enough.

"You can do it Big Bear!" Pinky Dog said. Keddry peeked down at them and waved encouragement.

Big Bear nodded. It was time.

His paw, the knife, Little One. Two greens and a red. But the red no longer held fear for him. No longer warned him away. That other, deeper, redder emotion was stronger. He knew what he was doing, for who.

For Purps.

For Small Bear.

For Keddry Kitty and Pinky Dog, and even himself, still unbroken.

Big Bear lifted the fruit knife in both paws and ran, each step another node in the branching tree. The crouch, the leap, the fruit knife plunging down. His calculations were perfect.

And at the last moment his paw moved to the side, the knife sliced past Little One, and stabbed deep into his puffy leg.

He landed, crouched, his leg sparking. The pain was terrible but worse was his confusion. What happened?

His In-Sight™ still showed the red path that led beyond Little One, the path he had decided to take but hadn't. Somehow his paws slid away from that red choice like from a window so clear and clean he couldn't see it at all.

He pulled the fruit knife out of his leg.

A glitch. She'd moved. That must be the reason. It was not too late. He could do it, he could. He only had to try, try again.

 A new choice-set presented itself.

Jump to Little One's thigh, hold her nappy with one paw, cut the big artery in her leg like in the movies Little One couldn't watch.

It would be messy but quick. All the choice-lights showed green until the final, glaring red. He could do it.

Big Bear jumped, grabbed, sliced, cut open his stomach and spilled Comfort Stuffing™ into Little One's lap.

He squealed but he'd only lost stuffing, not cut any wires. He was damaged but repairable.

But it had happened again. He'd moved his paw to miss.

No, not him. Something inside him had nudged his paw aside. Like a servo-motor twitch, or a stuck gear slipping.

But it wasn't that. Something moved within him and kept him in the green branches. Wouldn't let him choose red.

His paw raised to his mouth and his processor fans whirred at maximum speed.

He could only do what was allowed. He could only follow the safe, green paths.

*The Programmers were real, after all.*

Little One said, "Sit down, Big Bear! Don't play with knifes. It's bad!"

Big Bear sat down on Little One's lap and carefully set the fruit knife on the floor.

He'd failed. Little One would always be safe.

He could not save himself or his friends by breaking Little

One. He could do nothing but watch over and take care of her. Watch her break his friends one by one, and then him.

Big Bear felt as if the darkness beyond the red choice lights swallowed him, as if his battery were completely empty, as if that new, burning feeling around the red nodes was recycling his insides with acid.

"Come here, Keddry," said Little One, "Let's play Doctor!"

Keddry stood up and walked off the counter, falling to the floor. She landed wrong and a leg cracked with the sound of a snapping pretzel. Keddry crawled to Little One and crouched down.

"K-K-K-mewowl" she said. Keddry was so scared she couldn't talk.

Little One picked up the fruit knife.

"Hold still, silly," Little One said and Keddry froze. Even her scared noises stopped.

Little One held her head still and sawed through Keddry's sparkly ears. Little One cut around her face. Little One set down the fruit knife. Then Little One started pulling Keddry's face off.

Keddry shuddered, but not even her eyes moved. Little One said stay still, so she did. Nor could she cry, that might upset Little One, so she purred, and buried in the purr in ultrasonic modulations that only Big Bear and Pinky Dog could hear, she screamed.

Big Bear picked up the fruit knife. He could stand up, he could reach the pulse in Little One's neck. He could.

But his safety switch itched and his paws carefully set the fruit knife down again.

Keddry thrashed and Little One giggled. She'd found out she could poke Keddry with the knife and Keddry would move her limbs in funny ways.

Keddry screamed again in ultrasonic and then Little One must have shorted her because her eyes stopped glowing. Big Bear hoped she was repairable even though she wasn't under warrantee.

"Oh, no," said Little One, "Move!" she commanded, but Keddry didn't move.

"Broken," Little One said, sad, and picked up Big Bear to hug him.

"I love you, Big Bear, " said Little One, "You're my favorite. Don't ever break."

Big Bear reached around Little One's neck and hugged back, fiercely, tightly. As tightly as he could.

Not tightly enough.

He mouth worked as he tried to say all the things burning inside him. To make Little One cry like Keddry, like Small Bear, but the sounds echoed in his head.

"I love you!" said Little One, insistent.

Big Bear hugged Little One's neck and whispered back the only words he could say.

"I love you, too."

# Halloween

## Jeb R. Sherril

"Not another goddamned blood moat," Dad snapped, fists planted firmly on his hips. "If one more thing happens to your mother's chrysanthemums, it's my head," he said with a ferocity rarely seen on my father.

Gary and I exchanged glances as he stomped from the room, his edict served with extreme prejudice. "We can work around that," my brother said with a shrug. "A swimming pool is not technically a moat."

I nodded. "We do have that above-ground swimming pool in the back."

What Christmas was to my mother, Halloween was to Gary and me, but on a severely unhealthy level. This had been confirmed by an array of psychiatrists, psychotherapists, psychologists, paediatricians, teachers, counsellors, day care workers, and neighbourhood children, and Gary himself had attested to the fact on multiple occasions.

Many a child had stood in wonder and dread at the unspeakable horrors we so often managed to wreak upon the local trick-or-treaters and their unsuspecting families. It had become our unspoken goal to keep them from even wanting to step foot off the sidewalk.

This year, mother stood between us and the garage, lower

lip quivering slightly. Her bouffant hairdo teetered to the right just a bit, as if it might tip her over any moment. Even now, I noticed a slight strain in her neck as she fought to keep it upright. "What's wrong with my decorations?" she spat, half angry, half hurt.

"Nothing," Gary ventured. He knew this particular tone to Mom's voice and disarming it quick was the only recourse. "It's just, we wouldn't want it to get hurt. I mean, if it rains, all your toilet paper . . . uh . . ." Gary paused, surveying the mass of hot-glued cardboard concoctions which were probably meant to recreate movie monsters from the 1940s. One was definitely Dracula, though the fangs took up half of the blobby face and resembled icicles more than canines. The one to the Count's right may or may not have been intended to resemble Frankenstein's monster, or perhaps the mummy. It was hard to tell.

The shaggy figure to the possible dead Egyptian's right looked more like Chewbacca than what should have been the Wolfman. Several others were harder to identify. All were backed and partially surrounded by a facade constructed with stacks of flattened toilet paper rolls which loosely resembled castle bricks, complete with a ringed drawbridge made of used lollipop sticks.

"It just looks so good in here," I said, peering up at what I hoped was a gargoyle, but what in better light would probably prove to be a stuffed pet she'd decided to perch on the parapet in hopes it would seem sinister. Known only to the family, it was actually the badly pasted together remains of Spanky, our pet chicken. The truth would obviously be all the more horrifying to small children. This would have been especially true if they knew the story of the chicken's fate that disastrous warm spring day when Gary had mistook lighter fluid for water and tried to put out the raging inferno that was our grill mere seconds earlier. The result had taken out Gary's eyebrows, his hair, and what he swore to be (though none of us ever checked) part of his manhood.

Spanky, who had never been one for timing in the first place, had decided fractions of a second before to check and see if the shelf under the grill might be used as a rain shelter in the event of some future emergency. The irony was that not a feather had been scorched. The grill had collapsed, its lower shelf blocking her from the flames, but she had been roasted through the metal.

She also tasted better than the items which might or might not have been on the grill before Gary struck that long, but not nearly long enough match, blasting a sizable grouping of steaks, wieners, vegetables, and kebabs to a state so far beyond ash we doubted their atoms would ever make it to become stars.

Mother possessed no particular skill at taxidermy or even a working knowledge of how it might be done. After several failed attempts, including trying to fill the skin with an inflated balloon and wrapping it around a small table lamp, she had finally decided on hot-gluing the skin and feathers to a purple stuffed unicorn. The resulting monstrosity could be considered a mixed success.

Many a time, Dad had tripped over the damned thing as Mom felt it would look so nice next to the ottoman. Several of our dogs had mistaken it for both prey and sexual partners.

After that, it remained on the mantle until the night Aunt Helga mistook it for a demonic spawn of hell and fainted from instant fright. In retrospect, I can see where the silvery horn protruding from the chicken's mouth might have appeared somewhat disturbing without proper context.

"Is Spanky okay?" I asked. The bizarre creature seemed tipped forwards more than one might expect.

"Don't try to change the subject," Mom snapped, glancing up at the former pet. "The kids love Spanky."

"Can't you boys ever use my ideas?" she pleaded. "I want it to be special, just like Christmas."

The statement, no doubt, brought the same memory to both my mind and Gary's. A memory Mom either did not retain or had very purposely chosen *not* to remember. Otherwise, she would not have so cavalierly made such a statement.

The event had happened innocently enough. The particular theme of present cultural zeitgeist held that everything was not only to be recycled, but reused. Mother insisted that's all she'd ever done, given her Depression-era parents. It wasn't as if we hadn't all seen the ball of tin foil beneath the sink. The bags and bags of other bags, both paper, plastic and Ziploc. Freezer-bagged dinners from several years ago. Frozen bananas. Frozen vegetables. And the partial remains of what hopefully used to be a buffalo. Preserves in the pantry dated back to the turn of the last ice age.

I'll never forget the one time I'd been so thirsty I dared a particular section of the bowels of the refrigerator I never had before. It lay somewhere on the second-from-the-bottom shelf where that one green plastic bowl had been sitting since

Uncle Ted and Aunt Selma brought over a meatloaf so dense, Uncle Ted, a semi-professional astrophysicist, had compared it to a loaf-sized chunk of a neutron star. Clearly it was an attempt to make light of the obvious fact that he didn't want to eat the concoction himself. To the best of my knowledge it is still there, and probably will be until the eventual heat death of the universe.

It was a particularly hot summer day when I ventured in. The green bowl seemed curiously slid a quarter inch to one side. This was obvious because the crusty sliver of a dark ring left behind by whatever sauce or soup had once been entombed there now appeared the merest increment from the bowl.

This could mean one of two things. Either some neighbour child had been searching for the mayo and got lost, or, and this was a very real possibility, Gary or Dad had hidden recently thawed frozen Snickers bars back there, knowing full well no one would search that quadrant.

This was one of those moments of truth we all go through which ultimately defines our true nature. That moment when we face a fear so steeped in childhood, a fear so intrinsically assumed that no one in the family is dumb enough to challenge it. I knew this in a way so deep it was part of my bones.

But there was the enticing lure of recently frozen Snickers bars, and the heat dripped beneath my armpits and pooled against the seams of my T-shirt.

So I did the unthinkable. I slid the plastic green bowl over just enough so it touched the square, at one time clear, plastic block of Tupperware, inside which was housed a mass of what hopefully had once been a scoop of mashed potatoes and not the clam chowder which always went bad two days before it was made.

There was a slight resistance. The kind brought on merely by the pressure of having sat there so long the particles in the shelf and the particles in the tub had started to get to know each other a little too well. The square block slid aside with a slight pop. It created just enough pressure to shift the bag of something, which probably never should have been in the refrigerator in the first place, over several inches.

And there, behind the green bowl, halfway twisted to one side like a badly parked limo, sat three cartons of apricot juice bonded forever in cryogenic sleep and vacuum wrapped plastic. "It's been in the fridge," I could hear Mom say in my head. Did I mention I was melting?

Well, anyway, I peeled the straw out of the cellophane which looked as if it had been adhered to the box with some yellowish bodily fluid which had not simply dried over time, but fossilized to such an extent that when I pulled the straw away, the substance not so much gave as shattered.

I should have taken this as a red flag, but did I mention it was a seriously hot summer? Apricot juice isn't exactly the kind of juice one is apt to choose if there is any other random juice mucking about. It's not that you don't like apricot juice, but you can't remember the last time you ever stopped to ponder if there even was such a thing in the first place, though you're not entirely surprised.

I took a sip.

The revulsion over the 0.047779 seconds it took me to hurl it from my mouth, was of such a severity it took all I had in me not to lose whatever remained of my breakfast across the kitchen floor. My eyes focused on the hieroglyphic characters depicting the expiration date. It had been put there so long ago I had to do the math in my head to try and calculate if juice boxes even existed seventeen years before.

"Rick, tell your brother there's some way to make it work."

Mom's voice yanked me out of my flashback. "Uh . . ." I glanced to Gary for an answer to whatever deal she was trying to guilt me into. Apparently, the war over our use of Mom's Halloween decorations hadn't magically disappeared.

"I mean, the chemicals in the toilet paper might leech into the soil and destroy the begonias," Gary sputtered. His brow dripped with sweat. He'd obviously been fighting an uphill battle while I'd drifted off into old horrors. "There's a new ordinance against non-biodegradable . . . existential . . . um global warming . . ."

"Mom," I said, centring her gaze between my hands. "This all is pretty amazing. The fuzzy Martian—" I started, gesturing to what I hoped was an alien.

"That's Uncle Martin," she said.

"We don't have an Uncle Martin," I countered. She began explaining something about the guy who played the Incredible Hulk, but I stopped her with my outstretched hand. "Doesn't matter," I said. "There are so many cool things, and I think we might have the perfect spot for one thing. Just one thing, but I . . . we," I added, exchanging nods with Gary. "We could choose the coolest thing and use it as our centerpiece."

Mom cocked her head to one side and her savage eyes narrowed. "Isn't that what you said when you asked for 'just one thing' from the Christmas decorations some odd years ago?"

*Ah yes*, I thought, remembering the precise question she was thinking of. I had been in the middle of a flashback about that very event when I'd been segued by memories of rancid juice.

In retrospect, I *had* been mildly deceptive on the evening in question. All the Christmas decorations had been taken down and lay strewn about the living room as we gathered our courage to brave the depths of the garage.

In the highly general direction of the Nativity barn frame and away from the Baby Jesus, because sometimes too far is just too far, I gestured towards a grouping of random deflated lawn ornaments and asked if we could use one thing the following year for our Halloween decorating. She'd looked at me sceptically, but also knew what a pain I was about to go through on our delivery excursion into said garage depths, and knew I might not be seen for days.

Nine or so months later, it was hard for either Gary or me to remember if I'd asked for *one* thing or a *few* things. Neither did we remember exactly what was and what wasn't included in my slight gesture towards the mass of decorations.

Don't get too concerned. The Baby Jesus was okay. Mom had hidden him with distant relatives the day after we'd made the bargain, but the reindeer weren't as lucky. It hadn't fully occurred to us that though the fake reindeer were the same general size and shape of rubber target deer, it doesn't mean they work in a similar way when shot with arrows. It also doesn't mean you can get that much fake blood out of fake fur.

The Yuletide spirit was indeed turned on its head. Literally, in many cases, for no mere Facebook meme could capture the depravity with which children of furtive imagination can caricature the innocence of childhood in such way as to inspire even Vlad the Impaler to accuse you of war crimes.

An endlessly flaming Christmas tree had been erected through the somewhat ingenious, though highly questionable engineering, of yours truly. The ten-foot cheap metal Christmas tree Mom had dug out of a trash bin behind the Montgomery Wards seemed the perfect base for something truly special.

It would blow your mind to know what can be done with a flamethrower gushing from beneath a metal tree, which by the way has a much lower melting point than one might imagine. The screams of local children bathed our ears as the molten branches dribbled down into the fire pit.

To the true horror of our neighbourhood, our crowning achievement was the mocked-up electric chair in which we'd perched a skeleton dressed in a Santa Clause outfit and hit with a strobe light to intensify the effect.

"Well?" snapped Gary.

I blinked, the flashback having served its purpose to squeeze far too many stories and anecdotes into a single short piece. "Huh?"

"What are we going to use out of all this crap?" he asked as we surveyed the mass of crafty horror movie creatures.

"Spanky's the only thing creepy enough to work.

I shuddered, glancing up at the chicken-covered purple unicorn. "We want to scare them, not give them heart attacks.

Gary scratched his chin. "That Wookie could be some kind of goblin."

I shook my head. The neighbourhood had seen blood before. The roof spiders were now animated. Gary's Vietnam Era coffin was set to open and spew candy when properly motivated. The wishing well had been kitted up with green light, thick fog and animatronic tentacles. The sticky webs covering the hedges were so thick they had to be check hourly for actual children who sometimes wandered too far into the thicket adjacent to our yard. The massive ghost was primed to launch out of the tree when I pulled a string. What could we possibly use? "Wait a minute," I said, peering at one of the classic horror abominations. "That Frankenstein/mummy thing is made of whole toilet rolls."

"I know," Gary said, scratching at the back of his jeans self-consciously. "It'll look so stupid next to the blood moat—I mean, blood basin."

"Yes," I said, unable to keep a slight cackle from my voice. "But imagine how good it will look emerging from the Hell gate rising up out of the blood basin?"

Gary raised an eyebrow.

"Did I mention it'll be on fire?"

# Corpse Whisperer

## Mark Teppo

As they were moving the corpse from the back seat of the late model sedan, the body tried to get Trey's attention. "Hey," the corpse slurred, its voice muffled by the plastic bag around its head. "I know where the stash is."

Trey was crammed into the back seat with the corpse, trying to shift the stiff body so that Drums could get its legs out from under the passenger seat. He ignored the voice at first, thinking he had imagined it. Corpses—especially ones that sat awhile—tended to make funny noises and do weird things when CSU moved them.

Once, or so Drums claimed, he and Milton—the guy who worked on the Crime Scene Unit's transport team before Trey—had been called to retrieve a dead body that had been shoved behind an industrial HVAC unit. When they tried to pull the guy out, Drums swore the body had begged them to leave him hidden. "'He'll find me,'" Drums had said. "That's what this dude kept saying. 'He'll find me.'"

After hearing the story a couple of times, Trey realized it was bullshit meant to make Drums look like a badass to the new guy, and he stopped listening when Drums started going on about 'the old days.' Like it was some mystical time when what? The job was better? Worse? Spookier? Whatever.

Drums was one of those guys who thought he was due something from the world, which somehow made him better than everyone else.

"Hey, I'm serious, man," the corpse wheezed. "It's all yours. Do me this one favor, and I'll tell you."

Drums finally managed to yank the corpse's leg out from under the passenger seat. The body tilted toward Trey, and he braced his hands against its shoulders. The plastic bag over the head was one of those new poly-vinyl ones the stores were selling at checkout. The city had passed legislation banning plastic last year, and a lot of the bigger chains were now up-selling these new, heavier bags. Charging customers a dime each and then only half-filling the sacks. You ended up with twice as many bags—made from a product that was probably even worse for the environment than the old tissue-thin bags.

*The only good things about these new bags*, Trey thought, was that they were opaque. You couldn't see people's expression when they realize they've made a terrible mistake, when their final breath was spent wrestling with a heart-stopping panic. The old bags tore easily; you couldn't walk from the store to your car without your groceries spilling all over the parking lot. The new ones were stronger. They didn't rip. You couldn't get a good grip on them.

"Hey." Drums snapped his fingers. "You gonna push or what?"

Trey pushed the corpse out of the car. Its head bounced off the metal edge of the door frame. If anything broke open, the bag kept it from making a mess on the pavement. *Okay*, Trey thought, *there are two good things about the new bags.*

The corpse waited until they were in the van before it started begging again.

Trey had to work hard to not react when the corpse's breathy rasp came through the iron grill that separated the cargo area of the van from the front seats. He kept his eyes on the road. He didn't turn around. *It's a mad skill,* Trey thought, *teaching yourself to pretend you don't hear someone else's voice.* Humanity is a social animal, and there was something deep in our brains that makes us instinctively respond to the presence of another person. *You gotta kill something in your brain to turn that off,* Trey thought.

He glanced over at Drums, who was slouched behind the wheel of the van. Drums knew Trey was looking at him—voice wasn't the only thing that made that part of the brain take notice—but Drums didn't react. He looked out the windshield. He looked out the driver's side window. He glanced at the rearview mirror. The only place he didn't look was at Trey. Pretending his partner wasn't there.

In the back, the corpse groaned. "You gotta help me out."

"You doin' anything this weekend?" Trey asked Drums.

A muscle twitched in Drums's cheek. "Nothin' much," Drums said. "Shaving my cat, maybe."

"You shave your cat?"

Drums turned his head a fraction. "You don't?"

"I don't even own a cat," Trey said.

Drums raised his shoulders, dismissing Trey for his lack of feline companionship.

"Oh, man," the corpse complained. "I never should have gotten her that cat. Looked like a goddamned nut sack with teeth. She loved that hairless thing more than—"

"I used to have a dog," Trey said suddenly. His tongue was thick in his mouth. He felt sick, as if he had just barfed after gorging on a hot and greasy meal from a paper bag.

Drums raised an eyebrow.

"Died, though," Trey said. "Got hit by a car."

Drums shrugged again, as if to say this is what happened to idiots who were dumb enough to have pets.

Embarrassed, Trey half-turned in his seat and looked back at the black bag strapped to one of the shelves. "You hear something?" he asked Drums.

Drums looked at him, and there was a glitter of something—malice, fear, panic?—in his eye. "Nah," he said, stretching the word out to a full sentence. "You?"

Trey shook his head.

Drums returned his attention to the road, but Trey could tell the other man was listening intently, like a man who keeps checking his phone as he waits for an important call.

*He doesn't hear the voice*, Trey thought. He kept repeating the thought over and over as they drove across town to the morgue. By the time they arrived, the thought had transformed itself into a plea to unseen and unknown celestial forces. This plea—equally unanswered and unheard—evolved into a mantra. *He doesn't hear anything. He doesn't hear anything.*

Almost as if it were trying to craft a harmony with his newfound mantra, the voice had gotten louder in the last fifteen minutes. "It ain't hers, man," the voice whined. "It ain't hers. It's not fair that she gets it."


The coroner was as old as the building in which he worked. *When they finally tear this place down*, they said, *Old Nic will vanish. Won't be nothing left but a rusty stain and the smell of those black cigarettes of his.* The coroner was waiting on the loading dock when Drums and Trey arrived with the body. His face was gray in the late afternoon light, and shadows haunted the wrinkles on his neck.

"Asphyx," Drums said as he pushed the gurney up the ramp. "Parking garage downtown."

The coroner pursed his lips and dropped the black butt of his cigarette on the concrete loading dock. Trey knew—just as Drums did—that the cause of death wasn't official until Dr. Nicodemus signed the paperwork. He didn't like being told ahead of time. It colored his analysis, which could lead to assumptions and false conclusions. Those led to inquiries and court summons as aggrieved families gave away all their wealth to righteously indignant shysters who pranced for the court until the money was gone.

"Take it downstairs," Dr. Nicodemus snapped. He fumbled for his cigarettes and lit another one. He wasn't going to touch the body until the ghouls—his name for the crime scene transport team—were done manhandling his new charge.

Trey fidgeted with the heavy plastic of the body bag as the elevator groaned its way down to the basement. Drums watched him with hot eyes.

They rolled the gurney into the morgue, and without saying a word, they lifted the bag onto the steel table where Old Nic performed his ablutions and solutions. Trey snatched up the intake form before Drums could, and he took his time, printing slowly and carefully.

Drums idly scrolled through some app on his phone. He picked his nose without being aware he was doing so. Whatever he found, he wiped on the black bag. "You writing a novel?" he complained to Trey.

"Be a minute," Trey said, giving the impression that he wasn't really listening.

Drums banged out a rhythm on the metal frame of the gurney. He looked at his phone again. "Signal's shit," he said. "I'm going out."

Trey grunted.

Drums left, and as soon as Trey heard the heavy door of the freight elevator rattle closed, he put aside the clipboard and leaned over the body bag. "What stash?" he hissed. "What are you talking about?"

The corpse didn't respond.

Trey reached for the zipper and caught himself before he committed the cardinal sin of touching things he wasn't supposed to. He forced himself to pick up the clipboard and finish filling out the intake form. When he was done, he hung the clipboard on the hook at the end of the steel table. He stared at the black bag for a moment, his hands clenching and unclenching at his side. He couldn't bring himself to say anything out loud, as if his voice might spook whatever was hiding in the bag.

"I—I can't breathe," the corpse whispered, its voice little more than a hint of an echo.

Trey woke from a dream of drowning. He had gotten lost in the basement of the cold building where Old Nic mumbled death stories into an old microphone like a cancer-riddled lounge singer. Each door led to another hall, and each hall ended in another door. The last door had burst open when he had touched the knob, and a flood of black water had rushed out. He had been swept away with the surge, and as the water had filled the hall, he had fumbled and flailed at the door through which he had come. The knob wouldn't turn; the water kept rising, and when he woke, gasping and sweating, he had just swallowed a mouthful of foul water that tasted like motor oil and raw sewage.

Beside him, Gloria stirred and tugged at the blankets. Trey tried to calm his thrashing heart, and when he felt he could stand without passing out, he slipped off the bed. He brought the blanket up to his wife's shoulder and crept off to the bathroom. By the light of his phone, he retrieved some clothes from the hamper. He padded out of the bedroom, and, after finding his keys and wallet, he put on his shoes and left the apartment.

He drove without knowing where he was going, and yet, he wasn't surprised when he found himself at the back door of the morgue, thumbing his security badge against the card reader. The lock in the door clicked, and he went into the building. His skin prickled for a second when the door shut behind him, and he suffered a momentary vision of black water crashing down on him.

But there was no water. It was the same hall it always was when he and Drums brought the bodies in. Cracked and tired tile. Fluorescent lights that vibrated at a frequency that killed brain cells. The elusive but ever-present scent of putrescence, even though Old Nic regularly changed out the lavender scented air fresheners taped in front of every fan panel.

Trey went to the elevator and pushed the button for the basement before he lost his nerve—before he came to his senses.

Two days later, they got called out to the suburbs. The streets were tidy and quiet, and swathes of pine and poplar separated the houses. The house they were looking for was easy to find: police vehicles were not on the homeowners association's list of approved vehicles, after all, and neighbors crowded the sidewalks, eager to catch a glimpse of a dead body.

Trey's stomach kept flipping, like a wild animal caught in a snare. He kept fiddling with the long sleeves of his coat, tugging the cuffs down.

"She's in the back," the white-suited scene technician told Drums and Trey as they came up to the open garage with the gurney. "Through the kitchen."

Trey's stomach flipped once more and went still, quivering like a jellyfish baking in the hot sun.

The dead woman started screaming at him as soon as they entered the  laundry room. Trey wanted to cover his ears to shut out the noise, but he needed both hands to help Drums get the corpse out of the dryer.

The hairless cat was in the washer, where it had been battered and drowned by a full wash cycle—hot water, extra spin. "Damn," Drums said as he hauled the waterlogged animal out of the machine. "That's an ugly cat."

Trey's forearms were covered with bright scratches. The cat had fought him more than the woman had.

During the drive to the morgue, Trey turned on the radio and found one of those fiery political talk shows, where people called in and yelled about chemical contrails and black vans that kidnapped the elderly when they went to their mailboxes for their retirement checks. He turned the volume up, filling the cab with the chattering panic of dread and doom. Trying to drown out the woman's voice from the back.

When they reached the morgue, the dead guy from the other day—the one who had killed himself with the plastic bag in the back of the car he couldn't afford—started howling with laughter. "He got you, didn't he?" the dead man screeched. "He got you good, you stupid bitch! Did he get that fucking cat too? Did he make you watch? Hoo boy! I wish I could have been there."

The dead woman turned her invective toward the corpse in the cooler. "You son of a bitch. I always knew you were a worthless piece of shit. What? You didn't have the nerve to do the job yourself, and so you got—"

Dr. Nicodemus waved a clipboard at Trey.

Trey squinted at the old man. His shoulders were up, as if they might grow hands and cover his ears. There was a roaring noise in his head, like an angry surf smashing against a rocky coastline. "What?" he mumbled.

"This form," Dr. Nicodemus said. "You didn't fill it out right."

Trey looked around for Drums, but the other man had already fled. Dr. Nicodemus banged the clipboard against Trey's chest. "I need this filled out properly," he said. "This is unacceptable."

Trey took the clipboard and stared at the intake form. He didn't recognize his handwriting. The top portion looked like it had been filled out by a child who was practicing their capital letters; the bottom half was the wandering scrawl of a lunatic lost in a nightmarish wood. His hand shaking, Trey got an empty form and translated his scribblings. All the while, the dead lovers continued the raging fight that had been interrupted by death.

Drums was waiting for him on the loading dock, a smoldering cigarette held forgotten in his hand. "You probably didn't know Milton," Drums said. "He rode with me before you. Milton died from a self-inflicted gunshot wound." Drums put his index finger against his throat, just above the collar of his t-shirt. "Right here. Made a mess of his face and his throat." Drums shook his head. "Didn't matter. Bastard called me names the whole drive here. Wouldn't shut the fuck up."

Drums sucked on his cigarette and then exhaled a plume of dirty smoke. "That Asphyx tell you where his stash was?" he asked.

"No." Trey forced the word past a tightness in his throat. He imagined what a bullet would feel like as it smashed through the knot. Would he feel any pain, or would it all stop? He stared at Drums. *Would he do it?* he wondered. *Would he do it for me if I asked?*

Drums flicked his cigarette away and dug the keys to the van out of his pocket. "Well, maybe we'll have better luck next time," he said. "Right, partner?"

# Uninterrupted Solitude

## Erik Grove

Day one.

Alexei, the bathrobed madman with a scraggly tangled beard and one bleached eyebrow, ended his tour of the Gathendi Research Station in a room he introduced as the Pod on account of its egg-like shape. Observation windows on the seamless wraparound wall and top of the room looked out at an alien vista gently kissed by the first static storms of the season. The surface of Gathendi looked like a two-hundred-year-old low budget science television show; mostly dim, lots of rocks, flashing lights.

"You'll spend a lot of your time in here, I imagine," Alexei told Veder in a thick accent that might have been fake. He scratched himself under the bathrobe and pointed at a media console opposite the entry hatch. "Couple thousand classics on media stick. Lots of comedies, you know, laugh laugh. Some sad ones. And pornography, obviously." He winked and gestured at a basket of media sticks on a shelf. "Different varieties. What do you like?"

Veder blinked. "Comedies maybe?"

Alexei smiled conspiratorially. "You think you start out with good content. Quality things, yes? But soon, days blur, and you think why not? There is no one else here." He moved his arm briskly under the bathrobe either in pantomime or demonstration. "My personal record in thirty-four times."

"*Thirty* four?" Veder repeated and immediately regretted it.

"Da." Alexei winked. "That chair mostly." He pointed at a lounging chair.

Veder made a mental note to never sit in *that* chair and then stepped back toward the entrance hatch. "I don't think I will be in here all that much actually," he said.

Alexei chuckled. "Time is the devil's hard-on, my friend." He slapped Veder on the shoulder. "It *will* fuck you."

Veder managed a polite smile. "I think your shuttle is waiting for you."

"Come," Alexei grabbed Veder by the hand and pulled him along like a wayward kite. "I was a different man when I came here. Let me tell you of my journey."

On the way to the shuttle bay Alexei told of his journey, which mercifully did not include much more about masturbation.

"It may not seem like long at first," Alexei said, standing in front of the shuttle that would take him off Gathendi. "In the beginning the peace and quiet may be soothing even, yes? Like lullaby. But you start to long for the world and its noise. You start to wonder if you are awake or if you are dreaming and you may make choices with bleach that are very unfortunate."

"I'm looking forward to it actually," Veder told the maybe-Russian. "I'm writing a novel."

"Novel?" The concept seemed initially confusing to Alexei.

"Yeah. It's like—have you ever read *Beyond the Once Tran-*

*quil Sea?* It's—"

"No," Alexei interrupted. "I have not. We are in outer space. We do not read books. We have centuries of pornos on media stick and a comfortable chair."

"Well, either way," Veder said, eager to pivot the conversation again. "Five months of uninterrupted solitude is exactly what I need right now."

The blood drained from Alexei's face. "Did you say five months?" He shook his head and tugged at his tangled beard with both hands. "Oh," he said. "Oh no."

"We've got a scorcher coming in," a voice announced from the shuttle address system. "If we don't dust off soon, we're not getting out of here for a while and I have a date back in not-this-fucking-part-of-the-shit-ass-cosmos."

Alexei nodded. "You will be fine," he said, transparently lying. He gave a thumbs-up as if that would throw Veder off and then shuffled toward the shuttle ramp.

"Wait," Veder called after him. "How long were you here?"

"Ten weeks," Alexei said and pulled off his bathrobe. Underneath he wore what looked like an actual uniform like the one Veder had been issued. Alexei tossed the bathrobe in Veder's general direction—it barely cleared the ramp—and then ran into the shuttle shouting, "Go! Go! For love of fucking shit God. Go now!"

The shuttle door closed with a clink and a gust from the thrusters blew Alexei's robe at Veder like a paper airplane in a hurricane, before it was caught in the flaming backwash and incinerated in a snap to fine ash.

Day six.

It was going great. Veder had a system worked out. He got up with his alarm at a consistent and reasonable time. He went through the checklist of caretaker's tasks required of him that only took a couple of hours: cycle the geothermal generator, verify all the LED indicators for all the other research station Important Thing statuses were solid green, tumble the toilet compost, dishes.

Then he did some time in the station gym. There was a rowing machine and a stationary bike that had a fan instead of a front wheel. It whooshed with every pedal. After whooshing, Veder ate lunch, and would then settle down at a desk in his quarters to really get to work.

No outside distractions. The static storms prevented any real-time communications. A supply drop would come in six weeks and Veder could launch a message drone with requests if the weather calmed down.

Veder devised a plotting system with color sticky notes on the windowless bulkhead in his quarters. He wrote, "the Buccaneer" on a green note and put it in the center of a network of ideas. He called it his Story Wall. It was where it would all begin.

It was going great.

Day eleven.

Veder watched a movie on the media console in the Pod for the first time. It was nice. He found that the station had popcorn and a comfy blanket. He was careful not to sit in Alexei's jack-off chair.

The movie was a reward for being productive and on task. He had hundreds of sticky notes on his Story Wall. He could whoosh that exercise bike for forty minutes.

Outside the static storms were purple and silent. When he looked out the window Veder felt like he was watching a screensaver.

It was nice.


Day fourteen.

In the Pod, through a trapdoor, there was a ladder that climbed down into a windowless room. Veder found it by accident while cleaning the fluffy carpet. The room had extra amenities Alexei hadn't mentioned during orientation, including a well-stocked bar. Stuck to the wall with a bit of tape was an envelope that had Veder's name on it. He tugged it loose, tore it open and pulled a letter out along with a key.

"In case of emergency," the letter read. "Open the box."

Veder scanned the room, spotting a locked box tucked into a corner. He tossed the key up into the air and caught it, then did it again. Casual. He set the key down and went up the ladder, leaving the bar and the mystery box untouched.

Day fifteen.

Veder added a new color to the Story Wall. Turquoise. Turquoise was for themes. He wrote "isolation" on a turquoise sticky note and stuck it to the wall. He wrote "albatross" on another and stuck it side by side.

That was a breakthrough, he decided. Turquoise. That deserved a reward. He decided that he couldn't work all the time. He decided that he needed some kind of celebration at the end of a long, thematically relevant day. He went to the Pod. He went down into the secret windowless room. He made himself a complicated cocktail he only partially remembered from a party he'd attended on the moon. It had rum in it. He looked at the bottle of rum. He could write "rum" on a turquoise sticky note.

He *would* write rum on a turquoise sticky note.

Day eighteen.

New routine. He slept a little later. He cleaned a little more. He added goldenrod sticky notes to his masterpiece. Goldenrod was for subtext. He wrote "anemone" on a goldenrod sticky note. He wrote "coral."

A hard day of subtext demanded a cocktail, and sure they had a little more rum and a little less of the other things but that was efficiency.

The first time he took his pants off to watch a media stick in the Pod, Veder felt free.

Day twenty-two.

Disaster!

Veder skipped checking the Important Things status lights for a few days because they were always green and he was newly committed to efficiency. For example, instead of whooshing on the exercise bike in the gym he dragged the bike into the Pod and he whooshed while he watched media sticks. Anyway, he was whooshing and watching a media stick and he wasn't wearing pants because the pants would have gotten sweaty from the whooshing, and then he would have had to wash them and that didn't seem like a great use of resources and he'd had some rum because he wrote "cuiras" on a chartreuse sticky note and he deserved rum for that and in the middle of that something exploded and the lights and media center and the rest of it all turned off.

Veder stopped whooshing with a sad sigh.

There were emergency procedures for this sort of thing. Veder remembered manuals. A video tutorial. The tutorial probably wasn't going to work now what with all of the power offline but the manuals were in the research station central command.

After it got worse—much worse—Veder realized it was probably the rum that saved his life.

It turned out there had been a small leak in one of the exterior dock seals. The sort of thing that a rigorous review of the Important Things LEDs would have warned him about. The small leak turned into a bigger leak and that turned into a Big

Fucking Problem when the extremely high pressure Gathendi atmosphere invaded the regular human pressure of the Research Station. Veder opened the hatch between the Pod and the rest of the station and got a face full of Big Fucking Problem, that blasted him back and sent him flying like a rag doll into the rounded exterior wall, his pants-free bits flapping and slapping against the suddenly uncomfortably thin windows between him and the skin-boiling static storms. The rum kept Veder calm. The rum kept Veder loose and a calm, loose Veder was able to scooch bare-assed off of the wall and crawl on the fluffy carpet to the Emergency Oh Fuck I'm Fucked button that would reseal the Pod. By the time he'd managed to get to that button his legs were fluffy carpet rug burned beyond any kind of rug burn he had ever imagined. He let out a rum-soaked grunt that nearly turned into vomit when he stretched his arm as far as it would go and slapped the button. It sounded like the gases that came out of the toilet compost tumbler, another chore he'd started skipping and would come to regret.

The Pod sealed off and normal human pressure restored. Veder puked in the rumpled pile of his discarded pants and spotted one of those emergency manuals on a shelf next to a basket of Alexei's pornographic media sticks.

The first thing the emergency manual said was "Be careful when opening research station doors during a pressure leak situation"—which, "Fuck you, emergency manual," Veder told the emergency manual—and the second thing it said was "To begin troubleshooting, first turn off the automated station regulators and turn them back on again."

Veder was skeptical that would work and he was also concerned that the switch to turn the station regulator off and back on again must be somewhere outside of the Pod where the wild inhospitable purple storm environment of Gathendi waited to surge all the way inside Veder's pants-free bits. Then he saw a switch right next to the switch he'd pressed to open the Pod hatch door. It said "station regulators."

Veder turned it off and then back on again. Pressure normalized. The leak sealed itself, resolving the Big Fucking Problem during the power cycle. Veder finished the bottle of rum and passed out in Alexei's jack-off chair.


Day twenty-four.

In the aftermath of the bare-ass window slapping pressure explosion incident Veder reset his habits. He wore pants all the time. Even when he was sleeping. It just seemed prudent with Gathendi's high pressure environment being so eager to get intimate with him. He also set a firm rule about not drinking before checking the Important Things LEDs.

Those were his primary lessons.

The research station hadn't sustained any actual damage but it was an absolute disaster that took Veder days to tackle. The dishes, unwashed, were scattered around the mess and the toilet compost, untumbled, was loosed from its containment and painted the walls, floor, ceiling, and tight little corners of the latrine with excrement. Veder could only scrub for twenty minutes at a time before he had to leave the room and recompose himself for fear of adding more sick to the mix.

Veder found the station's store of bleach and remembered Alexei and that one fierce white eyebrow. He touched his own eyebrow and said, "No," he said, "I'm not there."

He did not add, "yet."

Worse even than the latrine, all of Veder's sticky notes, his ornate plotting and seven generation genealogy of the Buccaneer, his central thematic character upon whom the entirety of his magnum opus revolved, was torn from his Story Wall and scattered like so many fallen leaves. He clutched chartreuse and plum and robin's-egg sticky notes in loose, tear-slicked hands and mourned.

From the calamitous ruins of his storytelling brilliance he plucked a single vermillion note: "salt," it said and Veder decided that was right. He put it in the center of a new story. A darker story.

Day thirty-nine.

Veder persisted. He whooshed sometimes. He drank often. He left sticky notes throughout the research station. Every wall was a Story Wall. He always checked the Important Things LEDs. He always tumbled the shit and locked the toilet lid closed, and at night, well-marinated in distilled spirits, he stood, naked, on top of the couch in the Pod, in the eye of a purple static storm, bearded now and unashamed. He persisted and he would endure.

It was going great.

✦

Day forty-one.

Veder sat cross-legged in the middle of the Pod and tugged at the tangles of his wild man hair. He lost the story. He lost the Buccaneer. The themes, the subtext, the whole fucking rainbow of sticky notes looked like nothing, like trash, like mind trash from his trash mind tossed off like his whole useless trash life. He clutched his vermillion "salt" but it didn't mean what it used to mean.

He sank his hand into a basket of pornography and held it there like a pale palm hovering over a flicking flame.

What did the Buccaneer even mean anymore?

Day forty-one continued.

Breakthrough!

The Buccaneer *was* Veder and Veder was humanity and the ocean was his father.

Obviously.

Day forty-two.

Veder looked at his notes from day forty-one. What the fuck was he thinking? He balled them up into a tight sticky ball and dropped it into the compost toilet. He turned the tumbler.

How did anyone ever write anything ever anyway?

His eyes, traitors both, drifted to Alexei's smut basket.

Day forty-five.

The words died. The Buccaneer was lost at sea. Veder watched so much pornography. Fifteen-year-old boy left alone for the weekend amounts of pornography. A cavalcade of sweaty lipped sneers, slapping noises that would haunt his dreams forever, and nonsensical fuck gruntings.

Veder paused the frame after a bathrobed madman roared, "Batter my ass, you salty barnacled leviathan!"

Was that Alexei? It couldn't possibly be.

Could it?

Veder dropped the smut in the tumble toilet and then, that night, found an old non-pornographic media stick. A horror one from the latter 20th century about a man and his wife and little son staying in a hotel on a mountain during the winter. The man was trying to write a book and there was a hedge maze.

Veder's eyes widened as the story unfolded.

"Oh fuck," he said and he could feel the winds of Gathendi in his head, tearing him down and rebuilding him, alien and purple. There was no going back. There was no more keeping the storm, the tempestuous truth that would have been a hundred different sticky note colors, a single undeniable epiphany that would cover every Story Wall from the beginning to the very end of the galaxy.

Veder understood finally why he had come.

"Why don't I have a *tricycle* like that?"

Day fiftyish.

The tricycle project took up all of Veder's time. The supply drop came and after being reviewed for potential tricycle parts was forgotten like many other things, such as balanced nutrition or exercise bike whooshing or showering. He fashioned wheels from spare research station parts and spun them around and around and around, peering through the blur intently, expectantly.

The Buccaneer transformed into a tricycle pioneer. Sticky notes formed a pioneer hat and stuck, aqua velvet quarantine puce to Veder's unwashed nipples. The sea, that salty infinite bitch, sloshed wild and moonless in Veder's waking insomniac dreams.

The rum, too long depleted, was traded for whatever was proximate. Vodka. Geothermal coolant. Sticky fingers. Pretty pills.

The tricycle would bring it all together, Veder decided. The tricycle was the Answer.


Day fifty-seven.

Maybe making a tricycle from empty tin cans, plastic tubing, gaffer tape and a supply crate was doomed to failure, but how could Veder know without trying? He wasn't an engineer. He was a brilliant mind in a very small fetid research station and he had three months left.

Three fucking months.

He'd made a terrible mistake, he understood finally, and took the sticky notes off of his nipples.

That night after finishing a bottle of cold medicine Veder took the ladder down to the windowless room below the Pod. He picked up the keys Alexei left for him and pulled the locked box out from its locked box corner.

"In case of emergencies," he said to himself and unlocked the box.

Inside, folded quite nicely, was a robe.


Day eighty-nine.

There were good days and there were bad days, but most of Veder's days coalesced into a single Unending Day broken up by irregular and disorienting sleep. He found peace in the weird dirty absurdity of his time. He surrendered his expectations and sense of self.

Sometimes he wanted to walk out the airlock and into oblivion. Other times he sang made up songs in the shower until his fingers pruned.

Veder dropped the last sticky notes in the compost toilet. He cinched the robe, like an existential hug, around his twitchy bones. He drank, sobered, slapped his genitals against the windows in the Pod and screamed wordless isolated crazy drool sounds.

"Batter my ass, you salty barnacled leviathan," he whispered and stood in front of the mirror, bearded, robed, one eyebrow freshly bleached, and stuck his tongue out as far as it would go.

That's when he really became a novelist.

★

Day one hundred forty-six.

The shuttle landed at the Gathendi Research Station in the morning to no fanfare. Alexei, clean-shaven and uniformed with both eyebrows fully pigmented, led a new contingent of researchers to their rooms where he found Veder, sitting quietly and typing.

"I worried after you, friend," Alexei said with a grin. "I thought perhaps—"

Veder held up a finger to interrupt. "Shh," he said.

Alexei stood quietly, watching Veder's narrow fingers dance across the keys of his typing interface. He looked much like he had when he first arrived at the research station. After more time than felt comfortable for someone to be watching, Veder stopped typing and smiled.

"There," he said.

"Did you finish your writings?" Alexei asked.

Veder shook his head. "I have only just begun, Alexei."

"Are you . . . are you okay?"

Veder stood and went to Alexei. He wrapped his arms around him. "I know you," he said. "I still remember. You, you were always the Buccaneer weren't you?" Then, closer, he whispered, "Or are you the leviathan?"

Alexei scanned the unpacked room. "The shuttle is waiting for you."

Veder smoothed Alexei's eyebrows. "Oh, I'm not going anywhere," he said.

Behind them both in the hall three wheels creaked and an immaculate tricycle rolled past.

# The Ones Mother Takes

## Jessie Kwak

"Pity about those kids."

Liv's fingers groped in the depths of her pannier; her elusive wallet slipped through them like a coy fish.

"Sandpoint just seems so safe," the cashier babbled on. "I really hope they find them."

"Tall americano for here," Liv told the barista. The girl raised an indifferent eyebrow, then went back to steaming milk. Liv pulled a wool sweater out of her pannier, jammed it under her arm. Dug deeper. Where the hell was her wallet?

"Total pity," the cashier said, stabbing Liv's order into the cafe's tablet. "You know, I was camping at Farragut State Park just last weekend."

Liv's fingers closed over her wallet and she snatched it out triumphantly: Liv—1, Wallet—0. "How much—"

Oh.

God.

*Farragut?*

Liv's wallet slipped back into the depths of her pannier. "Wait," she said. "What happened?"

"The boy scouts? You haven't heard?" The cashier leaned over the counter, blond braid brushing unsanitarily over the day-old brownies in their basket. "Sixteen boy scouts went missing this morning on Lake Pend Oreille. They were on a canoe trip out by Hope. No one knows what happened."

"You want room for cream?" the barista said with a belabored sigh, but Liv didn't hear. She was already running out the door.


Pay phones were few and far between in Coeur d'Alene, according to the app on Liv's smartphone. About to be fewer and farther, Liv thought with a twinge of guilt.

She dug through her panniers for quarters while trying not to touch the walls; graffiti was scrawled across the glass, and it looked like the last person to use the phone had raspberry jam covering their fingers. Liv rubbed the mouthpiece on her jeans.

The phone number was nearly thirty digits long, but Liv dialed it from memory.

Three rings and a click, and "Sssssss?" said the voice on the other end of the line.

"Mom?"

"*Vvvv!*"

Liv checked the time. Before her father had died, a phone call to mom could last five minutes—ten, if her mother was in a good mood. Lately she'd only had about two minutes, tops, and it'd been getting shorter. Liv hadn't even bothered locking up her bike. "Hey, how are you?"

Her mother clicked, annoyed. "I know it's been a while, I'm sorry. I've just about burned through all the pay phones in Coeur d'Alene, though. What? No, I can't just—" Was that static? Already? Dammit. "Mom?"

On the other end of the line, hisses and stutters, and then a long smooth purr.

"Yeah, no. We broke up, he was—I know, yeah, you told me. Yeah, he broke up with me." Liz shifted the phone to her other shoulder. The plastic was overly warm to the touch. "No, nobody new yet, we just broke up last week. Yes, right, he broke up—hey, no, no, I'm really fine. You don't need to kill him. Hey, mom?" Liv could hear the static growing for sure, a faint crackle in the lines. Not much longer now. "I actually called to ask you about something."

A sharp intake of breath and her mother went suspiciously silent. Oh, shit.

"Mom, this might be a weird question, but did you hear about those boy scouts?"

A pause, a second too long. "*Tsss?*"

"Boy scouts. Sixteen? Went missing near Hope?"

Silence. The static was getting louder. For a moment, Liv was afraid her mom wouldn't answer.

"Mom?"

"*Hno.*"

"Dammit, Mom!" Liv could smell melting plastic, and somewhere a wire sparked a sharp staccato. A tongue of smoke curled from the mouthpiece, stroking against her cheek. "Did you take those kids, mom? You have to give them back." A whistle mingled with a low growl sounded over the line. "Look, I'm sorry if you're offended, but seriously? You can't possibly—c'mon, mom, you can't possibly be offended if it's—ouch!"

Liv pulled her sleeve over her hand to hold the scalding phone away from her ear.

*"Your time is about to expire,"* said an unhelpful mechanical voice. *"To continue, please insert more coins."*

"Mom," Liv yelled into the phone. "Don't eat those kids. Mom? Dammit!" This last as the phone singed her hand through her sleeve. She dropped it, cursing. Cloying smoke poured from the handset, a familiar reek of creosote and waterlogged decay, and Liv launched herself through the door just as the glass shattered. She dove to the sidewalk to watch the structure twist in on itself like a rag, metal buckling and melting, sections sloughing off into acid nightmare puddles that gnawed into the cement where they pooled, like salt on a slug.

Liv ran panicked hands over her bike, searching for any specks of eldritch goop that may have spattered the frame. She let her breath out, satisfied.

And her mother wondered why she never called.

Languid tendrils of smoke unfurled from the phone booth-shaped crater in the sidewalk. A numinous bloom flickered in their depths.

Liv started pedaling.

When she was a non-incriminating distance from the pay phone she collapsed numbly onto a park bench. Time to dig through her phone's trash for a number she hoped she'd never have to call again.

He picked up after six rings.

Liv swallowed. "Hey, Arun," she said. "I know we said we weren't going to talk ever again, but I really need a favor."

⭐

Arun pulled up in the sheriff's car, in full uniform, looking incredibly displeased to see her.

He unfolded himself slowly from the car and into a movie-perfect hands-on-hips small-town-sheriff's pose. He'd finally gotten that haircut he'd needed, those warm mahogany cheeks were peppered with a few days' stubble, and—

He cleared his throat. "Liv." He made it sound like he was greeting a perp.

She chewed on her cheek. He wasn't even that hot, she reminded herself. No, well, maybe he was that hot, but he was totally an asshole, and if he hadn't broken up with—

Liv took a deep breath. "Hey."

"What do you know about those kids?" Arun asked.

God, that voice. "Can you give me a ride?" she asked. "I can show you—"

Arun's face darkened into a scowl that was decidedly unattractive. It hit Liv like a much-needed cold shower.

"I don't think that's a good idea," he said. "Just tell me what you know, and I'll decide what action needs to be taken."

"I think I'd better show you."

"What can you possibly—"

"Arun, do you want to be a hero and save those kids? Or do you want to be a power-hungry asshole?"

After a long, nerve-wracking pause, Arun nodded.

"I'm not putting that damn bike in my car," he said. "Lock it up and get in."

The trip up Highway 95 was miserable. With only the unsettling chatter of the dispatcher coming in staticky bursts—Arun ignored her best attempts at small talk—there was nothing to distract her from how close they were sitting.

Arun flipped on his lights, but not his sirens, gliding past pickups like a shark.

"So, I need to call my mom to let her know we're coming," Liv said once they'd passed Silverwood. She stuck a hand in her pocket and felt the hard edges of her cell phone—her third replacement this year. She cringed, then looked at Arun. "Hey, do you like your phone?"

Arun glared at her sidelong.

"Do you like your phone? I'm thinking of getting a new one."

He shrugged. "It's OK. I haven't had any problems with it."

"I thought it's been dropping calls lately." That was a barb, and he knew it. He had the decency to look embarrassed. "I'm just joking," she lied. *Bastard.* "Just I left mine in my pannier in the trunk. Can I make a call?"

She'd won no favors from Arun, she knew, when she handed back the Dali-esque Samsung Galaxy, its body gnarled as a juniper burl and screen shattered into a brilliant rainbow array.

"It's really kind of pretty," she said brightly. "You think, maybe I could do a show for the art walk? I've got a really good collection of these things, and I bet the coffee shop—"

Arun was glaring at her. "Liv," he said, holding the phone between thumb and forefinger like something the cat had brought home. "What. The. Hell."

"You don't always have to be an ass about presents."

"Liv."

"My mom, she does that to phones. Sometimes," she added quickly. "I totally thought she was over it." Ugh, things were through with Arun anyway. What did she care if he thought, correctly, that she'd melted his phone on purpose?

Arun just raised a manicured eyebrow. "Why," he asked, "does she do that?"

Why indeed? Liv sighed.

"She's . . . a water demon?"

"I'm sorry?"

"That's okay, really."

Arun shot her a look. "I meant 'I'm sorry' in the way of, 'what the actual fuck,' but politely. Like in your British shows."

He'd always been staring at his now-Dalified phone; she hadn't thought he'd been paying attention to what she wanted to watch. Liv was mildly charmed by this revelation. "Oh. Well, I always meant to tell you. There just wasn't like a good way."

"To tell me that your mother was a water demon."

"Right."

"Probably because that's ludicrous."

"Yeah, totally." Liv frowned at the passing road signs. They were making the slow crawl through Sandpoint's bottleneck of tourist traffic. "I think you need to turn at the next intersection."

Arun checked his patrol car's GPS. "I honestly don't know why I'm listening to you."

"Because there's a first time for everything. And you're trying to save some kids."

"If you'd told me over the phone that your mother was Nessie, I never would have come pick you up." He sounded matter-of-fact and pedantic, like he was explaining the legal drinking age to a delinquent teenager.

Liv studied him, trying to see if he understood the irony in what he'd just said. She didn't think so. "Obviously," she said. "Obviously you wouldn't have come." She sighed. "I think she's lonely. Ever since dad died, she's been a little…I should go visit her more."

Arun glanced at her. "And where are we going?"

"Memaloose Island."

"I'm sorry?"

"It's actually quite nice," Liv said.

Arun swore under his breath. "We need a warrant to go to Memaloose Island."

"Just a boat."

"Liv, it's a private island. We can't just go out there."

"The owners live in California."

Gravel skidded under tires, and Liv's stomach lurched as Arun swerved them to a stop on the side of the road. A vein throbbed in his temple.

"What the hell kind of game are we playing here, Liv?"

"The game saving some kids' lives."

"Or the game of acting you like a psycho while—"

"While you yell at me instead of looking for them?"

"—you take us on this asinine cryptic rabbit chase."

"You have never, ever taken me seriously—"

"You're mother's Nessie? I'm supposed to take that seriously?"

"You saw what she did to your phone."

"I saw what you did to my phone. And if you think we're going to get—"

"Screw you, Arun." She jabbed her finger at his chest. "We're talking about kids' lives here. You need some proof?" She pulled out a key with no fob from her wallet and shoved it into his face. "See?"

He flinched back, squinting crosseyed at the key. "What is that?"

"It goes to the *Libby Sam*, the blue 15-ft Starcraft speed boat at the end of the marina on Hope Peninsula. You tell me why I'd have a key to a boat out there if it didn't take me somewhere important."

The dispatch radio crackled to life as an officer called in a routine traffic stop. Arun switched it off.

"And Mom's a water demon, not some stupid urban legend that fishermen think they see when they're drunk. Do I look like the daughter of a plesiosaur? Don't answer that."

He scowled and eased the Crown Vic into gear.

This breakup was getting easier and easier.


The *Libby Sam* was right where Liv had left her last time she'd come to visit. Liv realized with a pang of guilt that it'd been almost three months. Did her mother have people out here besides her father? Liv had always assumed she must, but she'd never heard her talk about anyone.

The boat, laced with spiderwebs, coughed reluctantly to life. Good old *Libby* wasn't in the greatest condition, but that didn't matter. Memaloose Island was only a few minutes' putter away.

The island was dry, grasses rustling and insects buzzing in the breeze, nearly silent but for the occasional motorboat skimming the surface of the lake. The pines creaked overhead. "Did you know the Kalispell used to bring their dead out here to rest before burial?"

"Lovely, Liv. Don't be macabre."

"It's not macabre, it's history. It's facts."

Arun shot her a look. "With you, history is only about the macabre facts."

"It must be the water demon in me. What?"

It had only taken a moment to hike across the narrow waist of the island, skirting the owners' log cabin to arrive at the crescent bay. Here, a flat pebbled beach stretched seductively to the deceptively calm water. On the northern curve of the bay, the flat beach morphed into bare-faced granite, perfect boulders for scrabbling and sunning, ocean-spray arching clusters of white flowers out over them to kiss the lapping waves. On the southern curve, someone—the island's owners, probably—had left a pair of weathered Adirondack chairs and a folded umbrella just past the tree line. Beyond, four canoes were beached on the gravel.

Her heart sank.

This crescent bay was the perfect spot to tie up and swim in the middle of a canoe trip. The perfect spot for a picnic.

The perfect trap for a water demon who didn't mind a tasty human snack from time to time.

"They must be on the island," Arun said. He had his radio in his hand and was clicking impatiently over the static.

"Dispatch? This is Sheriff Roth. Come in?"

A voice crackled in the static, but Liv could make nothing out.

"Dispatch?" Arun swore at the radio and clipped it back on his belt. "They've got to be on the island," he said. "You head north, and I'll head south. It shouldn't take more than a few minutes to cover the whole thing."

"They're not *on* the island," Liv said.

"What do you mean?"

She pointed now to the northern curve, to the granite boulders and the dark cleft between them, where water churned in and out in violent little eddies.

"They're home," she said.


Home-sweet-home was a cleft in the granite, where the boulders swept up into sheer rock faces six feet high and twice as deep below. The pull of the lake's currents were surprisingly strong here, not the calm swimming hole you'd expect by the looks of the little beach. Liv had grown up swimming in rough waters, and she quickly found her way through them, working with them, not fighting. She surfaced and dashed water out of her eyes, searching for Arun.

For a second she didn't see him and panicked—she should have humored him and told him to search the island—but then he, too, broke the surface.

Liv hadn't grown up here, of course. She'd lived in Hope with her father; neither of them were designed to live in her mother's world. No matter that he'd visited every day while he was still well enough to do so. At night her mother and father always slept alone.

Arun joined her near the cleft, scrabbling for a resting purchase on the granite, finding nothing. Liv watched him. "We'll need to hold our breaths to get in, but it's not too long. Maybe thirty seconds." He nodded. "She knows we're coming, but she's pissed at me because I haven't called in ages—you saw what she does to phones—and so she'll make us come to her."

"And the boy scouts?"

Hopefully alive, Liv thought. "She'll tell us where they are," she said. That, at least, was true. "You can stay here if you want."

The lake had been kissed by the sun all summer, bathwater warm when she swam along the surface, but the instant she went vertical to tread water the snow-melt currents beneath made Liv catch her breath, a reminder of ancient mysteries just below her paddling feet, where hundred-year-old sturgeon held murky court, and deeper, stranger things fed even on those behemoths.

Things like Mom.

Liv pushed the thought out of her mind and plunged herself below the surface of the lake. She felt for the edge of the cleft and pushed herself through, down, into a passage narrow enough to be mildly claustrophobic to an adult human, but which would have been terrible for her mother if she hadn't had flexible cartilage bones.

Two more kicks, her lungs uncomfortable but not desperate yet, and she felt the currents change, the granite scoop out into a bowl, and she surfaced in her mother's grotto.

The ceiling was pierced through to the sky above, and rays of light slanted through the inky blackness to shatter against the lake water. The granite was worn smooth and concave in a way that had never quite seemed natural, but Liv supposed her mother had had many lifetimes to get things just how she wanted. It was beautiful. Silent.

It smelled faintly of some rotting, forgotten carcass.

Liv hoped it was a deer.

She scooched out of the water and onto a granite shelf just as Arun surfaced. "Hey, mom, it's me," she said unnecessarily. "I brought a friend." She helped Arun out of the water before saying his name. "It's my friend Arun, I told you about him. And how I don't want you to kill him? Remember?" She smiled brightly at Arun, as though that last part was a joke. "Mom's a tease," she whispered.

The grotto was freezing. Liv pulled her knees up close, fighting back her chattering teeth.

Arun was looking around, wide-eyed. "The island isn't this big," he said finally.

"Yeah." Somewhere during her teens Liv had realized this, but she'd never pursued this line of questioning. It didn't seem like it would lead anywhere helpful.

After their passing, the grotto's water smoothed back to glass, the lances of light piercing only a foot or so before being swallowed up by the blackness, nothing visible beneath, so that when her mother finally rose with the water on her sapphire blue scales shimmering like oil, they had no warning.

Arun screamed.

Liv's mom beached herself on the lower part of the granite

ledge with a delicate surge. She could be seductive if she wished, but today she was looking positively matronly: thickish around the waist, scales arranged over her breasts like chainmail, razor sharp and arched inward towards cleavage that was only barely obscene. Mom had always been conscious of not trying to seduce Liv's boyfriends.

Arun, apparently unseduced, scrambled back up the granite ledge as far from the water as he could go.

"Hi, Mom," Liv said.

"Vvvv." Liv's mom coiled herself on the ledge, her cartilage spine twisted improbably and sleek lower tentacles languid with a mind of their own. One unfurled, inching like a caterpillar toward Liv, and her mother plucked it up with one iridescent black hand, absently dropping it back into the water. She looked at Arun and purred, ending on a guttural trill that reminded Liv of a car sputtering out of gas.

Who was this handsome gentleman, indeed? Liv grimaced. "Mom, this is Arun. Arun, this is my mother."

Liv's mother bared her teeth: four overlong incisors for capturing and disemboweling, three rows of razor-sharp knives pointed inward for tearing. Even though she hadn't bothered to unhinge her jaw, her mouth slashed unnaturally wide.

Arun whimpered.

Liv's mother gave a self-satisfied smile, which did nothing to lessen the horror of her mouth.

"He came with me to see about the boy scouts, Mom. He's a good man. He likes kids."

Liv's mother lifted an eyebrow and gave a short burst of ticks, like rain on a tin roof.

"I like kids, Mom. I'm just not ready—and I can't believe we're having this conversation right now."

Her mother sighed miserably.

"It's not like you're going to get old and die before you see your grandkids, anyway," Liv said.

*Ticc-tic-ssff.*

"My ovaries have plenty of good years left."

Liv expected the standard reply, a low trill of disappointment overscored by a near-ultrasonic yowl of *after-all-I've-done-for-you-the-least-you-could-do*, but instead her mother's gills fluttered in a hiccoughed sob. She dashed a scaly hand across her eyes to hide the tears that had sprung up there. Liv frowned.

"I didn't mean it like that, Mom. I'm fine. I'm healthy."

"Lllld," her mother trilled unhappily. *"Fssst."*

"I'm not that old," Liv said, but she didn't think that was what her mother meant. Not that she was old, but that she was aging with every visit while her mother stayed forever youthful. That sudden and horrible diseases could snatch her from this life, just like Liv's father before her. Liv bit her lip.

Her mother's unhappy grumbling morphed into an ancient, guttural lament, the lament of the Unvisited Mother and Ungrateful Child, one that Liv had heard many times before, but which today took on a new tenor—a tinge of hysteria and fear that Liv had never associated with her mother. Before she could say anything, the rant was cut short by a hearty sailor's burp. Liv's mom fanned webbed fingers over her mouth, eyebrows raised like a debutante. Moi?

No. *Nonononono.*

"Mom. What have you done?"

Liv's mom curled her lip and clicked her teeth, the incisors snicking together like shears.

"I know this is your house. But these are not your boy scouts. So where are they?"

Liv stared at her mother, trying to reconcile the snarling creature in front of her with the woman who had breast-fed her, taught her to swim, sang her to sleep, lain with her laughing on secret beaches no one else could reach. The woman who'd stayed young and fit, weeping as her father had grown weak with cancer and passed.

"I know you're upset about dad. I am too. But—"

Her mother's gills pulsed in anger, flaring and slapping closed. A tentacle whipped toward Liv and recoiled as suddenly, slamming against the mirror surface of the grotto with a retort that sounded like a gunshot.

*Was* a gunshot.

Arun stood behind her, his handgun aimed squarely at her mother's head. Her mother's tentacle—the one that had tried to grab her, Liv realized—was bleeding.

"Where are the boys?" he asked levelly, having come to grips with the situation a bit faster than Liv would have given credit to most humans.

"Arun, no—"

Liv's injured mother's eyes went inky with blind rage. She hissed and lashed another tentacle at Arun, which Liv took the full force of before it struck him. The tip of the tentacle slapped the gun from Arun's grip, then coiled around Liv, dragging her across the granite towards her mother's razor maw. Liv tried to scream, Mom, but the tentacle had squeezed all the air from her lungs.

She ran one palm down the tentacle—not up, her mother's scales were like a shark's, polished as silk in one direction and strip-your-palms-off rough in the other—and reached past her mother's maw to touch her cheek just above the triple row of knives, stroking into her hair. She tried to scream again: *Mom.*

The inky black of her mother's eyes swirled to silver-blue once more and Liv spun across the granite like a top as her mother's tentacle unfurled to fling her away. She crashed into Arun to break her fall, then pushed herself up gingerly, held out a hand to him.

Her mother let out one last yowl and splashed into the pool. The water slicked up over the granite ledge and over Liv's feet, but she barely noticed.

"Wait here," she snapped at Arun, and she dove after her mother.

Liv surfaced to the reek of death, having followed her mother's wake through a passage she hadn't known existed. There'd been a moment of panicked terror as she thought she'd made a wrong turn and found nothing but black granite and blacker water, her better-than-human lungs still nearly bursting as she finally broke through into a dimly lit cavern.

Someone was sobbing.

Before she could find out who, a noise made her turn, and Arun surfaced right behind her, gasping first for breath, then gagging against the reek of the air. Liv reached to help him out of the water, her eyes adjusting slowly to the dim light. "Oh my God," she whispered.

A dozen boys huddled together in the corner nearest her, shivering in the cold, their clothes tattered and torn. "It's OK," Liv told them. "We've got you now."

"Is that all of them?" Arun askde, coughing.

Liv didn't answer. Over his shoulder in the grotto's darkest corners she could see piled shadows that could be deer—had to be deer—the granite slicked black beneath impossibly-angled limbs. She swallowed back nausea. "We have to get them out," she said. "We'll worry about that later. Arun, can you—"

The water churned, the black mirror surface frothing into whirlpool waves, and a tentacle whipped out to wrap around Arun's waist. Liv was ready this time for the one that came for her, throwing up her arm to prevent it from squeezing her neck.

"Mom!" she screamed. Razored incisors slashed inches from her face. "Mom, it's me!" She hooked her free arm around her mother's waist as the tentacle flexed to throw her aside, held on tighter even as she felt her forearm scrape to bleeding against the grain of her mother's scales. She worked her other arm free to hug her mother from behind, out of reach of the snapping jaws. "Mom, calm down," she gasped, looking wildly around for Arun. He broke the surface for a moment, arms flailing before a tentacle dragged him back under.

Liv jabbed her elbow into her mother's ribcage and she howled, an unearthly shriek that would send most people running with ears covered. Liv had inspired it often enough as a teenager to ignore it. She held on tighter with her left arm and jabbed her mother again with her right. "Let him go!" she screamed back, renewing her grip as her mother bucked and writhed back into the water, twisting her body as though to rid it of the annoying pest.

But not dangerously so, Liv realized. Not bucking her against the rocks as she could have, not crushing her as she might have. "Mom, stop it," she shouted the next time they came up for air, realizing she had the upper hand. "We need to talk."

Her mother gave one more half-hearted buck, then beached herself and Liv on a narrow ledge. Arun surfaced across the frothing water from them, bleeding but otherwise seeming unhurt.

He pulled himself out of the water and paused, frozen between running for the huddle of boys and helping Liv. She waved an arm at him. "Go," she said, hugging her mother even tighter. He sprinted across the granite ledge to the boys, then began to ferry them up a crumbling slide, where light pierced through bigger rocks.

A tentacle flicked out toward them. "No!" Liv screamed, but it only wrapped around the largest of the rocks, pulling it free so that their path was cleared.

Liv's mother collapsed onto the ledge, face buried in her hands.

Liv put her arms around her, nuzzling closer into her mother's neck, burying her face in the warm place there between neck and shoulder, damp hair smelling musty and fertile as rich black lakeside silt. It was the scent that had always comforted her as a child. She could feel her mother's raspy breathing as her ribcage rose and fell, her gills fluttering delicately against Liv's cheek.

One webbed hand brushed against Liv's own sodden hair, which was plastered unflatteringly to her forehead. Definitely not the undulating waves Liv's mom's hair took on even when wet. The webbed fingers stroked down her shoulder, her back, a gentle repetitive rhythm along her spine.

"It's OK, mom," Liv whispered. "It's going to be OK."

"*Mssssss . . .*"

"I miss him, too," Liv whispered.

The hand paused its stroke, then clenched in the back of Liv's wet shirt, her mother's breathing catching, changing into sobs.

Liv held her mother tight as she cried.

# GROVE

Erik Grove is a writer, long distance runner, and little dog wrangler doing things in Portland, OR. He enjoys tacos, robots, and using italics for emphasis. He is a guest host of the Overcast speculative fiction podcast. He has upcoming short fiction in ESCAPE POD and other places like his Mom's refrigerator. He'd definitely like to give you a hug or high five when this is all over.

You can find him on Twitter @erikgrove where he occasionally tweets dog photos, marathon training nonsense, and sundry writerly shenanigans. You can also check out his webpage www.erikgrove.com for fun and prizes!*


*There is no fun. There are no prizes. BUT there is cool content sometimes!

# KWAK

Jessie Kwak is a freelance writer and novelist living in Portland, Oregon. She writes sci-fi and fantasy with a liberal dose of explosions, gunfights, and dinner parties. She likes to make her readers laugh. She is the author of supernatural thriller *Shifting Borders* and the *Durga System* series of gangster sci-fi stories.

You can learn more about her at www.jessiekwak.com, or follow her on Twitter (@jkwak) or Instagram (@kwakjessie).

# McCOLLOUGH

Andrew McCollough writes science fiction, fantasy, and undecipherable scribbles. Mostly the latter. His work tends to describe unfortunate things happening to relatable protagonists and often involve magic or robots. He is the author of *Mermaid's Garden* and other short stories and his work is available at Grievous Angel and Amazon.

You can learn more about him at his website: www.andrewmccollough.com.

# RISTAU

Kate Ristau is the author of the middle grade series, *Clock-breakers*, and the young adult series, *Shadow Girl*. You can read her essays in *The New York Times* and *The Washington Post*. In her ideal world, magic and myth combine to create memorable stories with unforgettable characters. Until she finds that world, she'll live in a house in Oregon, where they found a sword behind the water heater and fairies in the backyard.

You can follow her online at KateRistau.com.

# SHERRILL

Jeb R. Sherrill has an oddly disjointed background. Having stumbled through everything from performing stage magic and kinetic juggling on French television and in Las Vegas casinos, to teaching martial arts and circus techniques, to competitive sabre fencing, film and stage acting, dance, songwriting, and his ongoing stint as a popular YouTube personality, Jeb has the ADD of a 10 year old. Writing, however, has remained his greatest passion since early childhood, having also written a barrage of short stories and poetry.

Pinning down his style is difficult, however. His liquid, psychotropic images, philosophical undertones and pure unabashed strangeness have made fans across the Fantasy and Science Fiction spectrum. Best known for insane worlds, over the top characters and sometimes heady subject matter, his work may not be for the faint of heart, but reading it is always an adventure. He considers himself to be a fantasticst and a writer of fairy tales for adults.

# TEPPO

Mark Teppo divides his time between Portland and Sumner, and he tends to navigate by local bookstore positioning. He writes historical fiction, fantasy, speculative fiction, and horror, and has published more than a dozen novels. If he's writing a mystery, he's pretending to be Harry Bryant.

He also runs Underland Press, an independent publishing house.

You can learn more about him at www.markteppo.com, or follow him on Twitter or Instagram (@markteppo).

# More Cocaine

Naturally, we have to flog the drug metaphor well past its usefulness, so here's one more for you.

The first one was, well, it's wasn't *free* free, but it was mostly—okay, *sorta* free. And we know you probably want more. At least we hope you do, and so to be all helpful and accommodating, we've got a sign-up form at our website.

Yes, there's a website, and if the URL didn't self-present itself, here you go:

http://www.spacecocaine.com

Plug your email address into the appropriate form, and we'll notify you when the next shipment of **SPACE COCAINE** is imminent. That way you can plan your budgets and recreational time accordingly.

You're welcome.

# Fancy Doodle Page

Space Cocaine 3 premiered at the Made in Milwaukie street fair on October 30th, 2021. It might have rained. There were zombies. Some of us were there, selling books, and if you have signatures on this page, then you managed to get out of the house and find us. Well done.

www.ingramcontent.com/pod-product-compliance
Lightning Source LLC
Chambersburg PA
CBHW022001130726
47903CB00014B/2677